JEFF FOXWORTHY

Hide!!!

Illustrated by Steve Björkman

BEAUFORT BOOKS
NEW YORK

Hide!!!
Copyright © 2010 by Jeff Foxworthy

Library of Congress Cataloging-in-Publication Data

Foxworthy, Jeff.
Hide!!! / by Jeff Foxworthy ; illustrated by Steve Bjorkman.
p. cm.
Summary: Children play a game of hide-and-seek. Illustrations contain hidden objects for which the
reader may search.
ISBN 978-0-8253-0554-2 (alk. paper)
[1. Stories in rhyme. 2. Hide-and-seek--Fiction. 3. Picture puzzles.] I. Björkman, Steve, ill. II. Title.
PZ8.3.F828Hi 2010
[E]--dc22
2010012519

For inquiries about bulk orders, please contact
Sales@beaufortbooks.com

For all other inquiries, please contact
Beaufort Books
27 West 20th Street, Suite 1102
New York, NY 10011
www.beaufortbooks.com
info@beaufortbooks.com

Printed at RR Donnelley in Shenzhen, China, June 2010.

First Printing

Author photo on back cover by David Stuart.

To my godson Jack,

May you find all the good things in life.

JF

For David, Kristi and Michael, of whom I am so proud.

SB

On a Saturday morning
Like many before
The kids were all restless.
In fact, they were bored.

Find: 1 Raccoon

It had finally stopped raining
After nearly a week
Then they had an idea,
"Let's play hide-and-seek!"

Rachel Green volunteered
To be the first seeker.
The kids said, "Count to 100
And don't be a peeker!"

Find: 1 Raccoon, 2 Spoons

There are choices to make
When you're trying to hide.
Should you get behind it?
Should you climb inside?

You don't have much time
To decide what to do.
You'd better hide quick
Someone's looking for you!

Find: 1 Raccoon, 2 Spoons, 3 Mops

Mary Beth Grace had a smile on her face
'Cuz she knew right where she was going.
She's well hidden, no doubt
Can you pick her out?
There's just a small part of her showing.

Find: Mary Beth Grace, 1 Raccoon, 2 Spoons, 3 Mops, 4 Flip Flops

A garden of flowers
Has magical powers
To help a child
Trying to hide.

"Can you help me please?"
Said Sue to Ms. Breeze.
"Of course, dear!
NOW, QUICK, GET INSIDE!"

Find: Sue, 1 Raccoon, 2 Spoons, 3 Mops, 4 Flip Flops, 5 Monkey Eyes

"Where to go?" thought Chris Cash
As he made a mad dash
To hide where he'd never be found.

When he saw the big tree
His heart leapt with glee.
To find him, don't look on the ground!

Find: Chris Cash, 1 Raccoon, 2 Spoons, 3 Mops, 4 Flip Flops, 5 Monkey Eyes, 6 Butterflies

Some people can hide much better than others
And that was the case with David C. Smothers.

He knew blending in was totally key
And he did it quite well, I think you'll agree.

Find: David C. Smothers, 1 Raccoon, 2 Spoons, 3 Mops,
4 Flip Flops, 5 Monkey Eyes, 6 Butterflies, 7 Trucks

Little Jack Lee was not tall, as you see,
And for hiding this helped him a lot.
When he saw it he knew just what he should do.
Take a look, can you find him or not?

Find: Little Jack Lee, 1 Raccoon, 2 Spoons, 3 Mops,
4 Flip Flops, 5 Monkey Eyes, 6 Butterflies, 7 Trucks, 8 Bucks

Being skinny's a plus
When you're trying to hide.
It gives you more options,
That can't be denied.

Cindy saw places
That her friends ran right by.
It's not easy to spot her,
Want to give it a try?

Find: Cindy, 1 Raccoon, 2 Spoons, 3 Mops, 4 Flip Flops,
5 Monkey Eyes, 6 Butterflies, 7 Trucks, 8 Bucks, 9 Colored Mugs

Jimmy Wiggins ran off
With an idea in mind.
As a hiding place goes
It was one of a kind.

On the side of his house
Was the place that he sought.
If he could stay still
He might never get caught.

Find: Jimmy Wiggins, 1 Raccoon, 2 Spoons, 3 Mops, 4 Flip Flops, 5 Monkey Eyes, 6 Butterflies, 7 Trucks, 8 Bucks, 9 Colored Mugs, 10 Goofy Bugs

Jill and Neil had a plan
And they did not delay.
The Taylors were having
A yard sale that day.

With so many things
Spread across the front yard
Finding places to hide
Wouldn't be very hard.

Find: Jill & Neil, 1 Raccoon, 2 Spoons, 3 Mops, 4 Flip Flops, 5 Monkey Eyes, 6 Butterflies, 7 Trucks, 8 Bucks, 9 Colored Mugs, 10 Goofy Bugs, 11 Hooks

Saturday was wash day
For the old Widow Binder.
Wendy knew that, so
They might never find her.

Find: Wendy, 1 Raccoon, 2 Spoons, 3 Mops, 4 Flip Flops, 5 Monkey Eyes, 6 Butterflies, 7 Trucks, 8 Bucks, 9 Colored Mugs, 10 Goofy Bugs, 11 Hooks, 12 Books

The Mulligans moved
Nearly two months ago.
With no one mowing the lawn,
It was starting to show.

There were weeds everywhere
And the grass was quite high.
To find Mikey Moore
You will need a sharp eye.

Find: Mikey Moore, 1 Raccoon, 2 Spoons, 3 Mops, 4 Flip Flops, 5 Monkey Eyes, 6 Butterflies, 7 Trucks, 8 Bucks, 9 Colored Mugs, 10 Goofy Bugs, 11 Hooks, 12 Books, 13 Snakes

Find: 1 Raccoon, 2 Spoons, 3 Mops, 4 Flip Flops, 5 Monkey Eyes, 6 Butterflies, 7 Trucks, 8 Bucks, 9 Colored Mugs, 10 Goofy Bugs, 11 Hooks, 12 Books, 13 Snakes, 14 Cupcakes

Then a giant rain cloud
Appeared in the sky
And in just a few seconds
Nothing was dry.

And everyone who was hiding
Went running for home
Except Tommy Smith . . .

Who was dry as a bone.